This Little Tiger book belongs to:

_____

_____

_____

For Bunny and her little McLamb x ~ B D

For Mum. For always making Christmas
so special ~ A W

LITTLE TIGER PRESS LTD,
an imprint of the Little Tiger Group
1 Coda Studios, 189 Munster Road, London SW6 6AW
Imported into the EEA by Penguin Random House Ireland,
Morrison Chambers, 32 Nassau Street, Dublin D02 YH68
www.littletiger.co.uk

First published in Great Britain 2020

Text by Becky Davies
Illustrations by Alex Willmore
Text and illustrations copyright © Little Tiger Press Ltd 2020

Printed in China · LTP/3800/3952/0521

2 4 6 8 10 9 7 5 3

Can You Find
SANTA'S
PANTS?

Becky Davies   **Alex Willmore**

LITTLE TiGER

LONDON

When you're tucked up on Christmas Eve,
Santa's getting dressed.
His beard is trimmed, his boots are shined,
his fluffy suit is pressed.

But this year something's not quite right.
His bottom's feeling bare . . .
"Help," he cries. "Emergency!"
He's lost his underwear!

Can you find Santa's pants?

There's spare pants on the washing line.
See? No need to worry . . .

But now **those** pants are taking off!
Catch them, Santa, **hurry!**

He races through the kitchen door.
"I saw them blow inside!"
Now, if YOU were a pair of pants
where do you think you'd hide?

The elves all bustle busily.
There's sugar in the air.
This kitchen's full of gingerbread
but no pants **anywhere!**

So Santa tries the stables next.
Time is running out!
"Don't mind me!" he mumbles
as his elves all dash about.

The reindeer's coats are glistening,
their collars bright and red.
"But no sign of my pants!" he cries.
"What can I wear instead?"

This wrapping paper's flimsy and . . .

. . . his sack is much too loose!
It's itchy scratchy scritchy.
"I need **pants**! It's just no use!"

So Santa calls his closest friends –
Penguin, Reindeer, Bear.
He whispers in a quiet voice:

"I've lost my underwear!"

"Emergency!" his pals announce.
"There's no time for delay!
You **can't** deliver Christmas with
your **bottom** on display!"

Can YOU find Santa's pants?

Now elves are causing chaos as
they hunt among the toys.
Through treasure chests and sailboats
made for little girls and boys.

They look under stuffed elephants,
and carvings small as ants.
On tables, shelves and windowsills
till - hang on . . .

Santa leads his gang of elves.
They charge out in the snow,
dodging skis and snowball fights,

"Catch them!"

"There they go!"

Up the icy mountainside,
till something craCkS and creeeaaks.
Uh-oh! Can you hear that sound?
"Watch out!" a penguin shrieks.

Everyone's a jumbled mess
of green and white and red.
But Santa cheers – he laughs and whoops.
His pants are on his head!

"All hands on deck now!" Santa cries.
"Quick – load the sleigh up high.
With Christmas magic on our side . . ."